A Bedtime Story for Beloved

HUDSON

By Suzanne Marshall

Why is this book blue? The color blue can improve a child's sleep. According to studies, the color blue…

- Promotes tranquility and relaxation
- Reduces anxiety and aggression
- Lowers heart rate and blood pressure

We wish sweet sleep for Hudson!

LiveWellMedia.com

ISBN: 9798851445583

This book is dedicated to

Hudson

who is loved very much!

Welcome to Bedtime, Hudson! *says the Bear Cub.*
It's time for us to slow our pace.
Let's rest our paws and take a break.

Welcome Bedtime! *says Hudson.*
I am glad it's time for sleep.
I feel great. My day's complete.

Goodnight Hudson, Sleep Tight.

Goodnight Hudson, *says the Horse.*
It's time to sigh a giant breath.
It's time to settle, yawn and stretch.

Goodnight, *says Hudson.*
I have done my best today.
I deserve my rest tonight.
When a brand new day begins,
I'll be fresh to start again.

Goodnight Hudson, Sleep Tight.

Goodnight Hudson, *says the Lion.*
It's time to enter the land of sleep
where rest is soothing and
dreams are sweet.

Goodnight, *says Hudson.*
Sleep is wonderful. This I know!
Sleep gives me strength to play and grow.
After I rest, I feel refreshed.
After I rest, I feel my best.

Goodnight Hudson, Sleep Tight.

Goodnight Hudson, *says the Monkey.*
It's time to nestle in your bed.
So hug a pillow and rest your head.

Goodnight, *says Hudson.*
In my bed I'm safe from storms.
In my bed I'm cozy warm.
In my bed I feel at peace.
In my bed I fall asleep.

Goodnight Hudson, Sleep Tight.

Goodnight Hudson, *says the Tiger.*
It's time to gently clear your mind,
relax, release, let go, unwind.

Goodnight, *says Hudson.*
Tonight I blow away my cares
like bubbles floating in the air.
As they float away from me,
I am cheerful, calm and free.

Goodnight Hudson, Sleep Tight.

Goodnight Hudson, *says the Leopard.*
Let's put away all noisy thoughts
inside a magic bedtime box.
Tomorrow we can set them free,
like butterflies into the breeze.

Goodnight, *says Hudson.*
Tonight I'll dream of fun
like playing in the sun
and happy times to come.

Goodnight Hudson, Sleep Tight.

Goodnight Hudson, *says the Raccoon.*
It's time to shift our attitude
toward thankfulness and gratitude.

Goodnight, *says Hudson.*
I'm thankful for family.
I'm thankful for me.
I'm thankful for smiles,
laughter and glee.

Goodnight Hudson, Sleep Tight.

Goodnight Hudson, *says the Leopard Cub.*
Goodnight to us, to me and you,
from head to toes and elbows too!

Goodnight, *says Hudson.*
Goodnight to my feet, even if they're smelly.
Goodnight to my chest and to my belly.
Goodnight to my funny bones and my knees.
Goodnight to every part of me.

Goodnight Hudson, Sleep Tight.

Goodnight Hudson, *says the Polar Bear.*
It's time for tenderness and love,
for sweet goodnights
and happy hugs.

Goodnight, *says Hudson.*
I give myself a butterfly hug.
I give myself a lot of love.
I spread my love here and there.
I spread my love everywhere.

Goodnight Hudson, Sleep Tight.

Goodnight Hudson, *says the Panda.*
It's time to shine your inner light
throughout your body
soft and bright.

Goodnight, *says Hudson.*
In the quiet of the night,
I fill up my heart with light,
top to bottom, left to right.
I am hopeful, strong and bright.

Goodnight Hudson, Sleep Tight.

Goodnight Hudson, *says the Fox.*
Let's breathe together slow and deep.
Let's breathe together for our sleep.

Goodnight, *says Hudson.*
I breathe in peacefully.
I breathe out 1... 2... 3.
I breathe in sleepily.
I breathe out 1... 2... 3.

Goodnight Hudson, Sleep Tight.

Goodnight Hudson, *says the Lion Cub.*
Are you ready for your sleep?

Goodnight, *says Hudson.*
I am ready for my doze.
I am ready for my snooze.
I am ready for my ZZZs.
I am ready for my sleep.

Goodnight Hudson, Sleep Tight.

Goodnight Hudson, *says the Koala Bear.*
Are you feeling sleepy now?

Goodnight, *says Hudson.*
I am calm and sleepy now,
like I'm floating on a cloud.

Goodnight Hudson, Sleep Tight.

Goodnight Hudson, *says the Dog.*
I wish you wonderful sleep tonight.

Goodnight, *says Hudson.*
I will sleep well.
I will sleep great.
I will sleep soundly
until I wake.

Goodnight Hudson, Sleep Tight.

Goodnight Hudson, *say the Kitty Cats.*
You are loved to the moon and back.

Goodnight
Hudson
Goodnight

Pictured above: Suzanne Marshall & Abby Underdog (the inspiration for Live Well Media).

About the Author: Suzanne Marshall writes to engage and empower children. Her books are full of inspiration and unconditional love. An honors graduate of Smith College, Suzanne has made it her misson to spread love through storytelling. Learn more at **LiveWellMedia.com**.

Credits: All artwork was edited by the author. Heart Cloud (Vlad Ymyr, Pixabay), Sheep (Pisuttardging1, Vecteezy), Bear Cub (Agnieszka Bacal, Shutterstock), Horse (Callipso88, Shutterstock), Lion (Tambako The Jaguar, Flickr), Lion Cub/Cover Photo (Ridzwan09, Shutterstock), Monkey (Elmer L. Geissler, Pixabay), Tiger (Tambako The Jaguar, Flickr), Leopard (Tzvook G), Leopard Cub (Tambako The Jaguar, Flickr), Raccoon (Anna-Lina Eggert, Pixabay), Polar Bear (Gerhard, Pixabay), Panda (SJ Travel Photo and Video, Shutterstock), Fox (Shingo No, Pixabay), Koala (Dominador, Pixabay), Dog (Wirestock, Freepik), Kittens (12222786, Pixabay).

Made in the USA
Thornton, CO
12/07/23 07:05:07

fc6c6e58-f3ab-48b7-aae5-196a0d7b3806R01